THE CRYSTAL CHILD

Barbara Wersba

THE CRYSTAL CHILD

drawings by Donna Diamond

HARPER & ROW, PUBLISHERS

J
W

The Crystal Child
Text copyright ©1982 by Barbara Wersba
Illustrations copyright ©1982 by Donna Diamond
All rights reserved. No part of this book may be
used or reproduced in any manner whatsoever without
written permission except in the case of brief quotations
embodied in critical articles and reviews. Printed in
the United States of America. For information address
Harper & Row, Publishers, Inc., 10 East 53rd Street,
New York, N.Y. 10022. Published simultaneously in
Canada by Fitzhenry & Whiteside Limited, Toronto.
First Edition

Library of Congress Cataloging in Publication Data
Wersba, Barbara.
    The crystal child.

    "A Charlotte Zolotow book"—Half t.p.
    Summary: A young boy is haunted by, and later falls
in love with, a crystal statue of a young girl of long
ago.
    [1. Statues—Fiction.   2. Space and time—Fiction]
I. Diamond, Donna, ill.   II. Title.
PZ7.W473Cr 1982   [Fic]   81-48643
ISBN 0-06-026392-X   AACR2
ISBN 0-06-026393-8 (lib. bdg.)

THE CRYSTAL CHILD

1

The crystal statue stood in the garden, among the roses. She had once been a human child, but now she sparkled in the early sun—the folds of her dress forever neat, her eyes staring straight ahead. Her mouth was sad and perfect, like a crystal rose. Her hands were firmly clasped. As the sun climbed higher, drops of dew shone on the statue's hair. Rainbow colors washed her face, and a rabbit, hopping across the lawn, came to a halt and gazed into the statue's eyes. There was no expression there—no pain, no happiness, no fear. The statue did not seem dead and yet she was not alive either. She had simply stopped somewhere, along the road of time.

Once this child had played in the garden, had

rolled a hoop along the gravelled drive that approached the house, and had sat on the large veranda drawing pictures. Once she had climbed the chestnut trees and hidden in the potting shed at the end of the lawn. That had been eighty years ago. Another family lived in the house now and no longer found it strange that a child of crystal stood among the roses. When friends asked them the origin of the statue, they could not remember. It had to do with some tragedy, they said, for the house had once burnt down. But the child had never been human. That was only a story that country people told—a myth, a piece of folklore.

Yet there were two who came to visit the child each day as though she were a friend. One was an old man who had been a gardener in the neighborhood long ago. And the other was a boy. The gardener came to visit the statue in the morning, and the boy came after school. They had never met, but drawn by something they could not explain, each came to gaze at the crystal child—

and the gardener, partly from habit, would clip away the rose stalks that brushed her dress. Standing in the early light, the man would stare at the child's old-fashioned clothes and buttoned shoes, her long hair and folded hands, and the past would come back to him like a clouded dream. To the gardener, this girl was a part of something he had lost and could not name. But unlike him, she would never grow old.

The boy was a different matter. Taking a short-cut to school one day, and crossing the lawn of the estate, he had come upon the statue and had stood transfixed. It was not just that the child was life-size and that she belonged to another era. His interest was roused by her face. The sculptured mouth was the most beautiful he had ever seen, and the eyes, though expressionless, seemed to hold depth and color. The nose was perfect and small, and the high forehead was aristocratic. He could not take his gaze from the statue and stood there for a long time, waiting for her to speak. At last he realized how foolish this was, and went off to school. But each day he found himself returning to the garden, and each day it seemed as though the statue might speak to him. He was fourteen and the statue appeared to be a girl of twelve. Yet whenever he was with her, the boy felt that both of them were older.

The sun rose higher. Dew burned from the grass and dried on the child's crystal hair. The rainbow colors left her face and were replaced by a steady light. On a distant highway, cars and trucks could be heard. Inside the house, a telephone rang. A neighbor's dog sprinted across the lawn, barking at pigeons that clustered in the driveway. Present and past swam together in the sun while the statue glowed.

The old gardener appeared and stood staring at the girl. She looked different today, as though she had moved in the night, and her mouth was not as sad as usual. After studying her for a while, he put these thoughts away and began to clip the rose stalks that were touching her crystal dress. He had never had a child of his own and sometimes pretended that the statue was his child. Gently, he talked aloud to her. Gently, he clipped at the roses.

By late afternoon the garden was deserted. The angle of the sun pierced the statue like a sword, and in the western sky clouds gathered. Birds fluttered in the chestnut trees, waiting for night. The statue's eyes stared straight ahead. A starling perched on the pedestal on which she stood, and for a moment both child and bird were trapped in time. Then the boy ran across the lawn, schoolbooks under his arm, and the bird rose into the air with a cry.

Placing his books on the grass, the boy sat down cross-legged and gazed at the girl. She was becoming a part of the sunset and clouds seemed to drift through her eyes. The autumn rose petals fell about her feet. "What will happen to you when it snows?" the boy asked. "Will you feel the cold?" He thought of the statue standing in snow as the wind whipped her face. He saw a white mantle covering her dress and hair.

Suddenly he longed to take her home with him, to a place where winter would not hurt her.

Hearing footsteps behind him, the boy turned and found himself staring into the eyes of the gardener. The old man had forgotten his clippers and had come back for them. For a second, neither the man nor the boy spoke. Then the gardener sat down on the grass.

"I come to visit her too," he said. "Been doing it for years."

"Why?" the boy asked.

"Don't know," said the gardener. "Don't know."

The boy felt that he did know, and that the old man had stories to tell. "I come here every day after school," he confessed. "Do you know who she is?"

The gardener gazed across the lawn. "Well, yes I do. In a way. But everyone has his own version of things. You know that."

"Who is she?"

After studying the boy, the old man seemed

to change his mind about something. "It's this way," he said. "I hadn't been born yet, at the time of the fire, but when I was growing up I heard stories about it. It seems that this girl here was an only child, very sensitive and delicate, and very close to her mother. The father loved her too, but it was the mother she cared about. You understand?"

"Yes," the boy said.

"They were fine people, real gentry, and the girl had everything. She had a governess, and a stableboy to look after her pony, and a big doll-house that stood on the lawn. Things were different then, you see. Life was different."

"Go on."

"You won't understand."

"Yes," said the boy. "I will."

"Well . . . when the girl was around twelve years old, a fire swept the house. She escaped, and the father escaped, but the mother was killed. And it had a terrible effect on the girl. For a long time she didn't cry. Not a single tear."

"Go on," the boy said.

"Well, as I say, she didn't cry. Couldn't cry. But one day her tears came, tears for her mother, and people who were there at the time said that the tears turned into crystal. And then the child herself turned into crystal. Right before her father's eyes."

The boy showed no expression in his face. "What happened next?"

The old man sighed. "What could happen? The father took his girl and placed her here, in the garden. Then he moved away and wasn't heard of anymore. The house was rebuilt and new people moved in, and then other new people. And so it went."

"How could the father leave her?"

The gardener rose to his feet. "Don't know. But she's been here for eighty years now, and will probably be here when you and I are gone." He shook his head. "Nobody believes this story, son. Nobody at all."

Stooping slightly, the gardener walked away.

And when twilight had drawn a dark veil over the sky, the boy left too. Only the statue was left behind—the crystal statue, who had heard every word they said.

2

The statue gazed at the garden. Roses had turned silver in the moonlight, and drops of dew lay scattered on the grass like jewels. In the center of the driveway the stone fountain splashed its water coldly. The world was hushed, yet vibrant. Everything seemed awake.

A white cat crossed the lawn and vanished into the bushes. Before it disappeared the girl saw that its eyes shone yellow, like little lamps. Her own cat was white too, and she had named it Snowflake.

Beyond her the house loomed in the silver light—its broad roofs shimmering, its windows glowing faintly. Her dollhouse, which stood on the lawn, was an exact replica of the mansion, complete with gables and a wide veranda. The house was large enough for her to stand in, and the dolls who sat on the sofas and chairs looked alive—some of them having tea, others staring out the window. Her father had built this miniature house with his own hands, and had even covered the walls inside with rose-colored paper.

The crystal child listened to the sounds of night—the voices of sleeping birds within the trees, and the notes of a piano within the house. She heard laughter coming from the servants' quarters on the top floor. She heard her pony, Valiant, whinny in the stable. She thought of the man and the boy who had talked about her earlier in the day, but the words they said were part of her crystal dream. For years people had come to gaze at her, and to talk about her, but she knew that she was only dreaming them. Her true reality was the house that glittered in the moonlight, and the piano music that drifted across the lawn.

It was almost nine o'clock. Her father would be reading in the library, as he always did at this hour—and her mother would play the piano for a while, and then walk through the rooms extinguishing lamps. The servant girls would gossip and giggle before retiring. Toby, the stableboy, would bed Valiant down for the night. At last the house would become a solemn sleeping thing—a giant who breathed under the stars.

The girl thought of her mother, and knew that of all the mothers in the world hers was the kindest and the most beautiful. She and her mother played together as though both of them were children. They shared all their thoughts, and on summer nights they would swing lazily in the hammock between the oak trees. "You are my golden girl," her mother would say, hugging Alison close. And at these moments the child would know that they lived in a world apart. The life of the house flowed over shining rocks, but she and her mother lived in the stream's center, secret and untouched. As

13

the piano music reached the child's ears, she saw her mother's small white fingers flying over the keys.

Then the clock in the stone tower struck nine. And the fire began.

It started in the nursery on the second floor, and at first there was only a flickering light in the window—as though a party were going on. Shadows danced gaily across the room, but soon all of the nursery windows were illumined with a steady orange glow. A crackling sound filled the air, like flags snapping in a high wind. Flames shot through the roof and up the chimney. The screams of servant girls could be heard as they fought their way downstairs through the billowing smoke. Alison heard someone cry out, "God! Oh, God!"

And now she was standing on the lawn in her nightdress, clutching her governess' hand. Sparks and ashes were flying through the air, and suddenly a ball of flame landed on the roof of her dollhouse. Within seconds it was burning too, and

Alison could see all the dolls burning inside, sitting on their chairs and sofas. The stableboy had released Valiant, and like a crazy thing the pony was galloping round and round the pasture. He's screaming, Alison thought. My pony is screaming.

The night was filled with bells—the bells of the fire wagons, and the bells of the town church which pealed steadily. Men were running across the lawn with hoses and buckets. Neighbors had gathered in small groups, talking, crying. Alison saw her father dash out of the burning house and knew that her mother was with him. She must be with him. He would not leave her inside.

The house had become a furnace. It leapt against the black sky, and crackled and roared, and there was nothing anyone could do to save it. Alison watched her dollhouse collapse in flames. She watched her pony gallop round the pasture like a mad thing. She felt her governess' arm about her shoulders and realized that she was trembling violently. The sound of the bells and the roaring house slammed against her ears.

And then she saw her father run into the house again and emerge seconds later with his clothes on fire. She saw a fireman roll him over and over on the lawn in a blanket, and realized that her mother was not there. Of all the people gathered together, the neighbors and servants and children, the village priest and the gardeners and firemen— of all these people, only her mother was missing.

She began to run towards the house, screaming, but was pulled back by her governess. Then, as the crowd on the lawn moaned aloud, she looked up to the nursery window and saw her mother standing there, her arms outstretched. She had gone back to find Alison, and now she was outlined in the burning window just as the dolls had been outlined in the windows of the dollhouse. Her mother looked like a giant doll.

The fire came every night to the crystal child. And every night the child would hear Emma, the upstairs maid, say to her: "Miss Alison, you mustn't keep leaving a lamp by the nursery curtains. Those curtains are so thin they'd catch fire

in a minute. Miss Alison, please try to remember."

But she had not remembered. And the small oil lamp with its pretty glass shade, the shade with Chinese ladies painted on it, had indeed ignited the curtains—and the burning curtains had ignited the world.

The statue saw these things and remembered these things, but since she was only crystal she had no feelings about them. And every night, just as the fire had come, it would disappear—leaving a crystal girl standing in the moonlight, two crystal tears upon her cheek.

3

The boy gazed at the statue. Once again the sunset was coloring her face and hair. Once again clouds seemed to drift through her eyes. Her silence was so great that it made the rest of the world clash with sound. Her crystal form was as empty as air. Yet the old man had told the truth yesterday. On the girl's cheek were crystal tears.

The boy had looked at the statue many times, but had never seen the tears. Nor had he noticed that her hands, which were clasped in front, were tense and strained. Her eyes said nothing, yet there was something in her that was trying to speak to him. He knew this as clearly as he knew anything in the world.

He stood on the grass and realized that he was

trembling. Why was he alive when she was dead? Why could he move so easily when she was trapped in crystal? He wanted to take her hand and lead her out of the garden. He wanted to feel her small hand warm inside his own.

"I love you," the boy said. And the words shocked him. "I love you," he said again, and the words took on rightness and truth.

He had never loved anyone before and believed people when they said that he was cold and unfeeling, that he spent his life in books, and that books meant more to him than reality. He believed them when they said that the only person he cared about was himself. But none of it was true. Love had simply been waiting to grow inside him, like a plant that has never felt the sun. And now he had fallen in love with someone he could not have.

The statue was dead. She stared into the sunset with cold eyes, and its colors were her colors. When the moon came she would turn into moonlight. When it was dawn she would become dawn for a while and sparkle with rainbows. She had no life beyond these moments. She was made of rainbows and the moon.

The boy felt his heart tighten as he remembered the dream he had had last night. In this dream he was walking through a museum—a place of stone walls and high arched ceilings. The halls of the museum were endless, rooms led into other rooms, yet he could find no sign of life. Fear gripped him as he heard his footsteps ringing on the cold floors. The museum was filled with priceless paintings, objects and jewels, but he was the only visitor.

He came to a marble stairway and began to climb it—but the stairs kept multiplying. No sooner had he mounted one stair than two more would replace it, so that he found himself running desperately to reach the top. Pausing, he heard an eerie sound beneath him. It was his own footsteps, echoing in the rooms below.

Then the dream changed and he was in a hall

of statues. The hall had no end and the statues went on forever, growing smaller and smaller in the distance. They were made of marble, stone and wood, and represented all of civilization— some of them Greek, some Egyptian, others from the Renaissance, and still others in clothes he could not identify. Many of them were warriors and had swords in their hands. A few were children who had been caught in moments of play. He wanted to leave these frozen figures, to turn and run away, but something held him there. It was their eyes, their endless staring eyes.

They want me to give them life, the boy thought. And this idea was terrifying, because he knew that if he brought them to life they might destroy him. Yet the temptation to wake them was irresistible. He began to walk down the line of statues— past an Egyptian king and a medieval knight, past a woman with a child in her arms—and finally came to a halt in front of a young Greek boy. He was around twelve years old and was dressed in tunic and sandals. Standing on tiptoe, the boy

kissed the statue's lips. Life came into its eyes and its body stirred. Smiling, it stepped down from the pedestal.

He proceeded down the hallway, kissing each statue on the lips—and as each came alive it began to follow him, waiting for him to breathe life into the others. Soon a dozen statues were following him, and then a hundred, but none of them spoke. All he could hear was the whisper of their clothes, the clank of their swords.

At last he saw the crystal child. She was standing on her pedestal as she had always done, her hands firmly clasped, her eyes staring straight ahead. And a surge of joy came into his heart, for he knew that he could free her. He paused in front of her, aware that the others were watching. They had formed themselves into a circle around him.

"You belong to me," he said to the crystal girl. The words filled him with love, and standing on tiptoe he kissed her crystal mouth. It was the first real kiss of his life, and for a moment he thought he could feel warmth in her lips, a faint stirring. But the girl did not move. Frantically he kissed her again, and then again, but she was lifeless and cold. "The others are awake!" he cried. "You must wake too!"

He could feel the army of statues moving in, circling closer and closer. Soon they were so close that he could feel their breath on his face and hear their ancient hearts beating. They began to speak, in voices that were terrible and inhuman. They sounded like animals.

They will kill you, the boy thought. If you do not wake her, they will kill you. No, his mind said, they will not kill you. They will turn you into a statue.

Then he woke.

Remembering this dream, the boy felt himself go cold. For the meaning was very clear. No matter how he tried he would never wake the crystal girl, and if he continued to want her he would become lifeless too. The love in his heart would turn to crystal. Eventually, he would die.

He stayed with her all that night, sitting on the grass at her feet, and the night was voices and stars. Unable to sleep, he listened to owls cry in the treetops and watched black clouds racing across the moon. The stars were a thousand eyes, staring at him. The house loomed in the distance like a sleeping giant. A white cat stepped into the moonlight, gazed at him and disappeared. Finally, at dawn, he put his head on his knees and slept. Waking an hour later, he looked at the girl and at the light which was shining through her.

The statue had changed. Her hands, which had been so firmly clasped, were now hanging quietly at her sides.

4

The gardener stood at a distance, watching the boy and the statue. The boy was standing in front of her with a face as white as a ghost's—and quickly the gardener saw why. The girl's hands were no longer clasped. She had changed in the night.

The old man had expected this to happen, but now he feared for the boy and for what it might do to him. The boy was young and did not know the mysteries that life held. And while the gardener did not know all of them, he did know that one day the crystal girl would move or speak. That was why he talked to her every morning. That was why he took care of her.

The old man stood quietly, his shoulders

stooped, and wished that he had told the boy the full truth two days ago. But truth and imagining were so close in his mind that he did not know how to talk about them. How could he have told the boy that he had often seen the child's mother crossing this very lawn? She was there every day—standing on the grass with a parasol over her head, swinging in the hammock between the oak trees, walking about the grounds. Both real and unreal, a vague transparency making her blend with the garden, she drifted through sunlight. The gardener thought that she was the most beautiful woman he had ever seen. Her long skirts and coiled hair reminded him of his own mother.

The boy was talking to the statue, and though the gardener longed to walk up to him and comfort him, some instinct kept him silent. The story would unfold as it had to unfold. He was powerless to change it.

Unaware that the old man was watching, the boy spoke rapidly. The words he said made no sense, and because he was tired tears came to his eyes. Now that the statue had moved he knew that he must reach her, touch her, rouse her into living. But he did not know how. The morning sun flashed coldly in her hair, like diamonds. A cold sky tinted her dress.

The boy thought of the life he and the girl could have if she would only wake. He saw the two of them growing up, loving each other and marrying. He saw them moving into the house and beginning life anew. They would have children, and just as the crystal child had played in these gardens and ridden her pony around the pasture, so their own children would do the same. Time would curve back on itself and the past would be redeemed. A dollhouse would stand on the lawn. The sound of laughter would echo through the trees.

For the first time, the boy reached out and touched the girl's face. It was cold. He stroked her hair and it was the same. She could have been made of ice, her body was so empty to his touch, so frozen.

The boy wept. He did not know that he was about to weep, but once the tears came there was no stopping them. And the thing that amazed him was that he was not crying for himself, but for her. Things that he had taken for granted all his life—movement, speech, books, music, animals— all these things were denied to the statue. She could not even feel the sun that was bathing her perfect face.

His tears fell on her hand. But instead of glittering there, like dew, the tears sank into her crystal skin. Then the boy saw the hands stir. Quietly at first, like flowers in the wind, the fingers trembled and moved. Color entered them and soon the entire statue was transformed. Instead of crystal hair, the hair was blond. Instead of a crystal dress, the dress was rose-colored cotton. The buttoned shoes were white leather. The sash around the child's waist was silk. As though a painter were stroking her with his brush, the girl became a creature of warm cheeks and blue eyes, pale hair and rosy cotton. To the boy's astonishment, she yawned.

She stepped down from the pedestal—and instantly the boy could see that she was at home. Her solemn eyes passed over the lawn, fastened on the place where the dollhouse had stood, and glanced away. She looked at the potting shed at the end of the garden and stared up into the chestnut trees. Finally, she looked at the house.

Pain came into her eyes and she uttered a little moan. And the boy felt selfish because his own happiness was so intense. It's all right, he wanted to say, I'm here, I love you. The sorrow in the girl's face silenced him. She stared at the house as though she could not believe what she saw. "My mother," she said.

It's over, the boy longed to say, it happened years ago. But the girl was crying now. He stood and watched her, his happiness fading like a dream.

She was sobbing bitterly, the tears pouring

down her face, and though a thousand words raced through the boy's mind, he knew that none of them were good enough. Her grief was so profound that nothing could touch it. Her memory was so sharp that it burned in her eyes like flame.

Without looking at him she began to walk towards the house—slowly, deliberately, placing one foot after another. "No!" the boy cried, but she did not hear him. She was walking towards the past, and time was curving back on itself to create a tragedy. The boy ran after her and tried to grab her arm. He could not touch her. Where flesh and blood should have been was only air.

She was moving closer to the mansion—and just as he was about to run after her again, the boy felt the gardener's strong hand on his shoulder. "Let it be," the gardener said. "Let her go."

The child was in the distance now, past the grape arbor, and as the boy and the gardener watched she approached the house. For a long moment she stared at its gabled roofs and shining windows, its wide veranda with the wicker furniture. Then she changed her mind and turned towards the pasture. The angle of the sun blinded the old man and the boy, and suddenly they could not see her. They knew that she was there, near the stable, but the sun was piercing their eyes.

"She's gone!" the boy said.

"It's all right," said the old man. "Wait."

The sun rose higher and the pasture became visible. Its long grass was swaying in the wind like silk. The red stable, with its worn paint, glowed softly. The morning was made of blowing grass and an old red stable, winds and gentle clouds.

Then the gardener and the boy saw the girl again, standing in bright light near the stable. She was talking to someone, and for a moment they could not make out who it was. A woman? Yes, it was a woman with long skirts and coiled blond hair—a graceful figure who had a parasol over her head. She was holding the child's hand and the two of them seemed to be laughing.

As the light grew more intense, the day began

to shine like crystal. Smiling, the gardener pulled the boy close and ruffled his hair. And the last thing they saw in the distance was a woman with a parasol and a child with buttoned shoes crossing the blowing grass.

They were walking into the sun.

Barbara Wersba is the author of more than a dozen books for children and young adults. Her last novel, *Tunes for a Small Harmonica,* was a National Book Award nominee, and in 1977 she was awarded an honorary doctorate from Bard College for her contribution to the world of children's literature.